NATHALIE DARGENT is a children's author, screenwriter, illustrator, and blogger. She lives in Paris. *The Christmas Feast* is her English-language debut. Visit Nathalie's website at nathaliedargent.com.

MAGALI LE HUCHE is the illustrator of *This Is a Good Story* (Simon & Schuster), *All My Friends Are Fast Asleep* (Farrar, Straus and Giroux), *With Dad, It's Like That* (Albert Whitman), and over 40 other books for children. She studied illustration in Strasbourg. Magali lives in Paris, where she often teaches art workshops for children.

For the Dragonfly.

—N. D.

To the band of Couderc children: Mathilde, Anna, and Clara,
and all the Christmas feasts they will have together.

—M. L. H.

First published in the United States in 2020
by Eerdmans Books for Young Readers,
an imprint of Wm. B. Eerdmans Publishing Co.
Grand Rapids, Michigan

www.eerdmans.com/youngreaders

Original title of the work: *Le Festin de Noël*
Authors: N. Dargent & M. Le Huche
© Éditions Glénat 2008

English-language translation © Eerdmans Books for Young Readers.

Manufactured in the United States of America.

28 27 26 25 24 23 22 21 20   1 2 3 4 5 6 7 8 9

Library of Congress Cataloging-in-Publication Data

Names: Dargent, Nathalie, author. | Le Huche, Magali, 1979- illustrator.
Title: The Christmas feast / written by Nathalie Dargent ; illustrated by Magali Le Huche.
Other titles: Le Festin de Noël. English.
Description: Grand Rapids, Michigan : Eerdmans Books for Young Readers, 2020. | Originally published in French: Grenoble : Éditions Glénat, 2008 under the title, Le Festin de Noël. | Audience: Ages 4-8. | Summary: "Fox, Weasel, and Wolf steal a turkey for their Christmas feast, but the meal has her own ideas about how to celebrate the holiday"—Provided by publisher.
Identifiers: LCCN 2019054596 | ISBN 9780802855374 (hardcover)
Subjects: CYAC: Animals—Fiction. | Christmas—Fiction. | Humorous stories.
Classification: LCC PZ7.1.D324 Chr 2020 | DDC [E]—dc23
LC record available at https://lccn.loc.gov/2019054596

The Christmas Feast

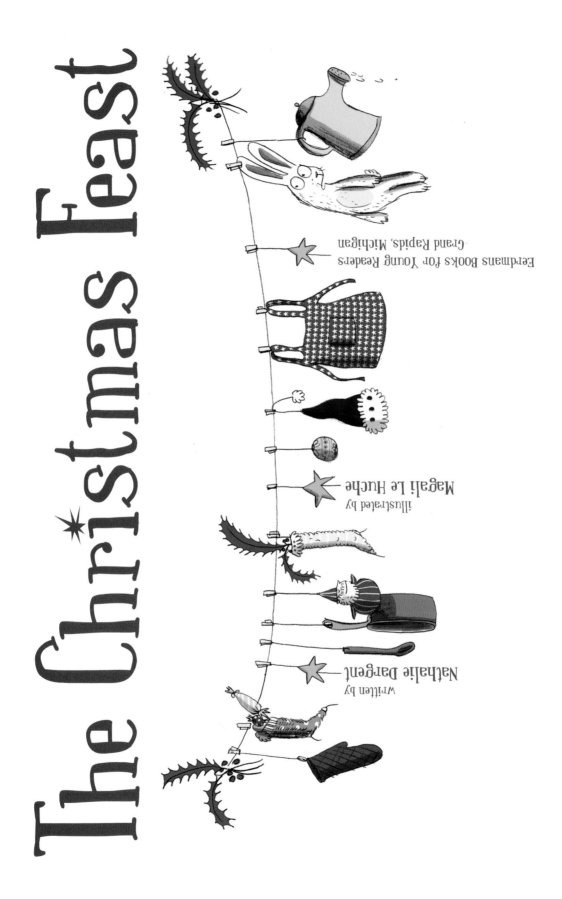

written by
Nathalie Dargent

illustrated by
Magali Le Huche

Eerdmans Books for Young Readers
Grand Rapids, Michigan

One year, the wolf, the fox, and the weasel decided to treat themselves to a Christmas feast.

Fox was in charge of stealing the turkey. And since he was clever, he went early to find the best-looking one. But the adventure got complicated once he returned to the burrow . . .

"Oh, what a mess it is here!" the turkey exclaimed, barely out of the bag the fox had stuffed her into. "Didn't you ever learn to clean up your den before inviting a girl over?"

"You're not my guest!" Fox protested. "You are my Christmas feast!"

"Even more reason to get rid of this mess! A Christmas feast is a big deal. You have to put some care into it. For starters, you need to clean things up and let in some fresh air. I can't stand untidiness."

And Turkey perched on the chair to oversee the work.

Grumbling, Fox got to work. He wasn't very happy about it—but this Christmas feast was quite sure of herself. When Weasel and Wolf came back later, the burrow was spotless. They were even asked to wipe their paws before entering. But as soon as they spotted the turkey, they cheered.

"Isn't it time for dinner?" Turkey interrupted. "I'm hungry. What did you make?" Weasel and Wolf licked their lips and replied that they didn't have any intention of cooking, except perhaps to turn her into pâté.

Turkey scolded them sternly: obviously, she needed to be fattened up before they ate her! Good grief, everybody knows that! Was this their first Christmas? Was this their first feast?

Ashamed of their ignorance, the three friends agreed, and then followed her instructions to the letter: Wolf went to gather sprouts, Weasel searched for mushrooms, and Fox fished for frogs.

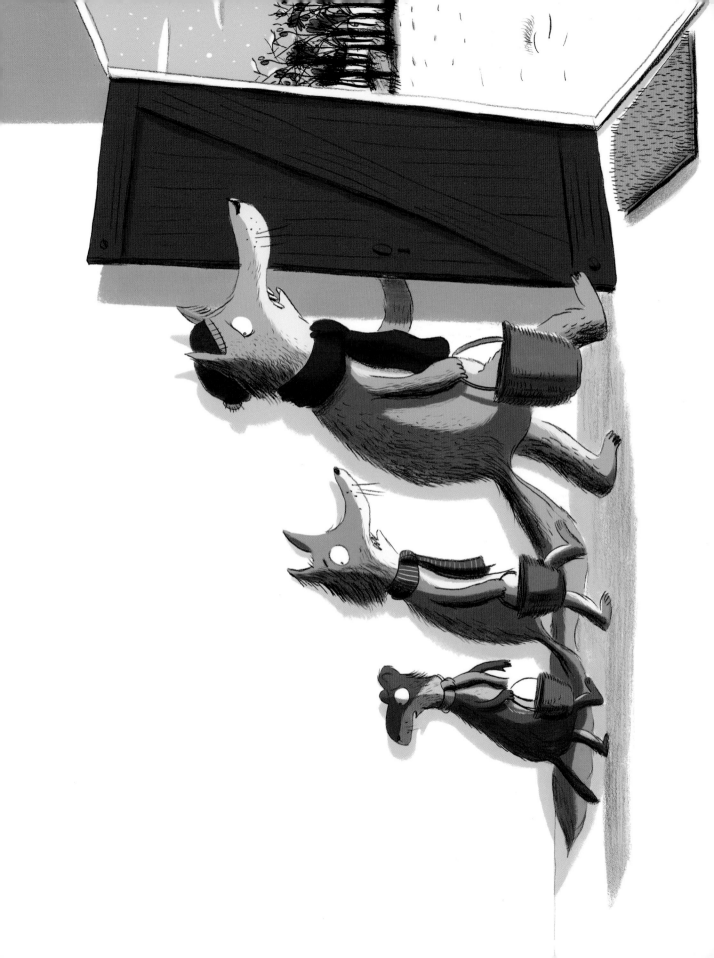

Since none of the hosts knew how to cook, Turkey prepared a frog and sprout stew with puréed mushrooms. They all enjoyed the food very much.

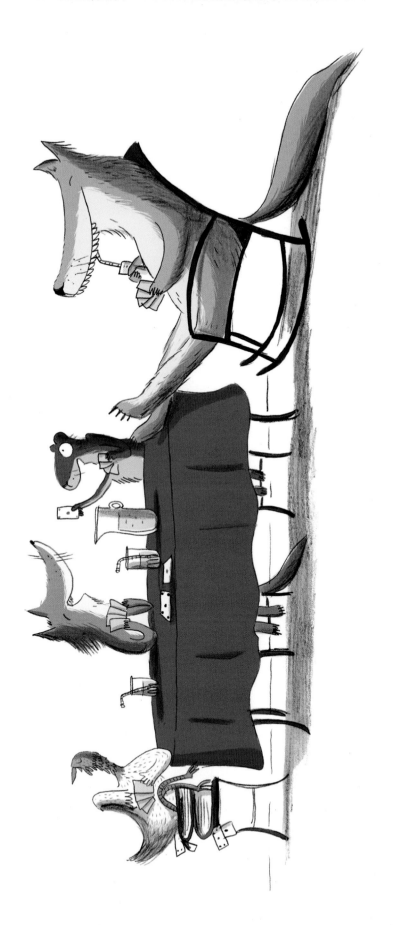

After dinner, they played cards—and because Turkey cheated better than all of them, she won. Still, the friends had a great evening, the best in a long time.

That night, they didn't have to fight over who slept in the armchair: it was only right to leave it to Turkey, as she herself had pointed out. They fell asleep wherever they could find room, after brushing their fangs as they were asked.

Turkey woke them up early the next morning: she was hungry. The three friends went searching for food, and Turkey made breakfast with what they brought back.

For the rest of the day—and the days that followed—the three didn't spend one minute on their own. Turkey was quite demanding, even between meals. She needed holly to weave wreaths, a Christmas tree to decorate, and bunches of mistletoe to hang from the ceiling. They also had to sweep the chimney, since Turkey was quite sensitive to the cold.

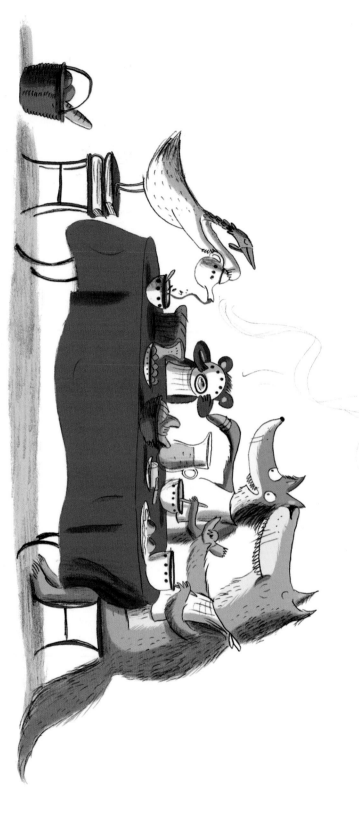

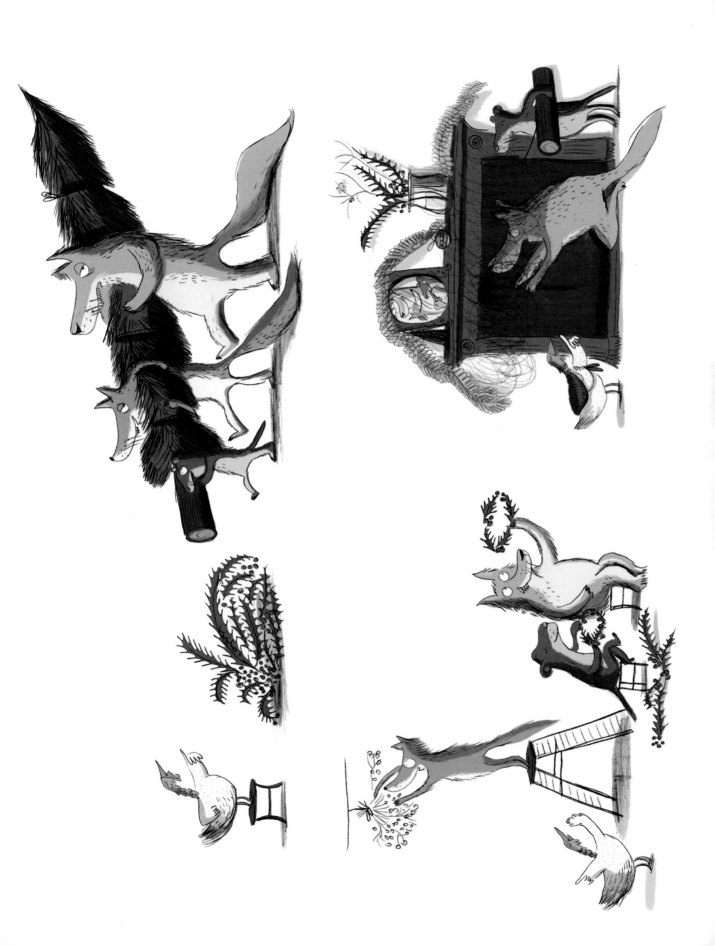

As Christmas approached, the three companions still washed their paws grudgingly before sitting down for dinner, but they had started to like all those good meals. They still didn't win at cards, but they knew how to make gingerbread and garlands. They found it was actually quite fun to get ready for Christmas!

On Christmas Eve, Turkey raised an important question: how would they cook her? Would they roast her and serve her with gravy? Stuff her with herbs?

"I would like to be flambéed," she requested. "But the recipe is quite difficult. Will you be able to manage it?"

The three friends let out an embarrassed cough. They hadn't thought about that. They postponed the conversation until the following day, and not one of them got a wink of sleep that night. They didn't have the slightest wish for their new friend to end up roasted, stuffed, or flambéed. But what could they do?

Fortunately, Turkey found a solution.

"Dear friends," she said the next morning, "I can see you're afraid that if you kill me too soon, you'll end up going hungry. Well, go ahead and fatten me up for another year. There will always be time to eat me next Christmas. I will be fatter then, and the feast will be even better."

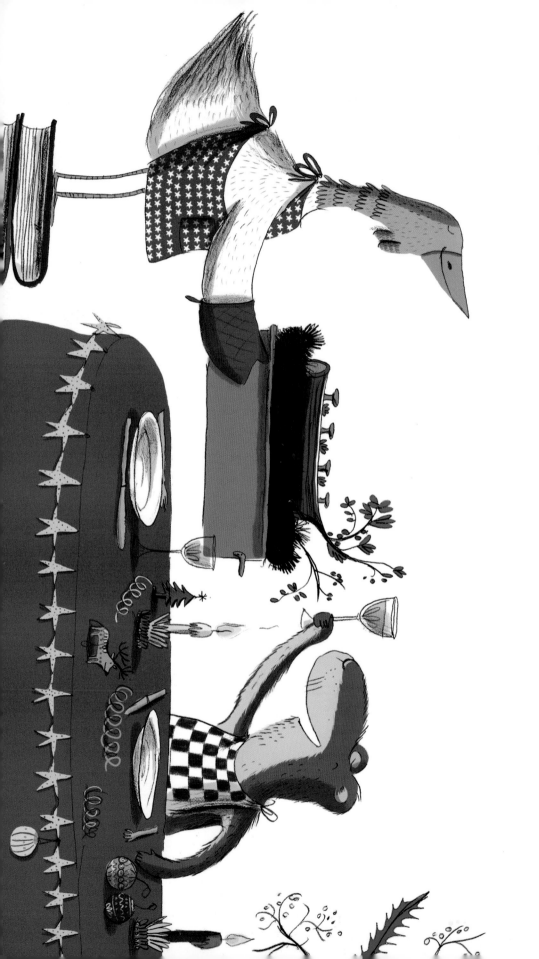

The proposition was accepted unanimously.

And so Turkey prepared the Christmas feast herself.

Once the animals had settled on this arrangement, they renewed it Christmas after Christmas. And since then, nobody in the forest has ever seen a burrow more joyful or a bunch of friends fatter and happier than Weasel, Fox, Wolf, and Turkey.

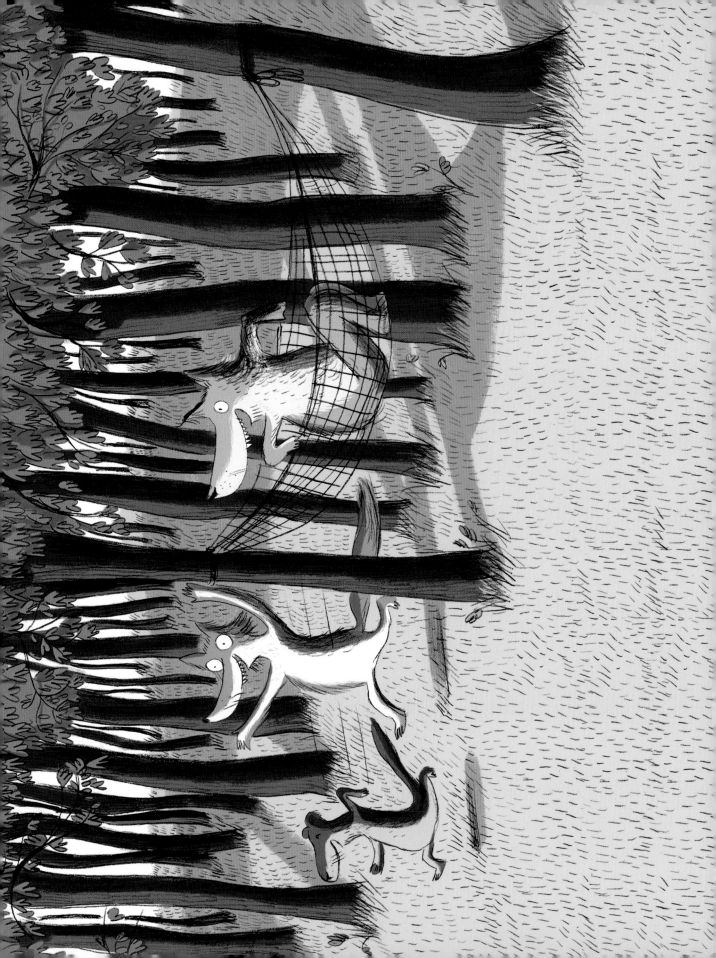

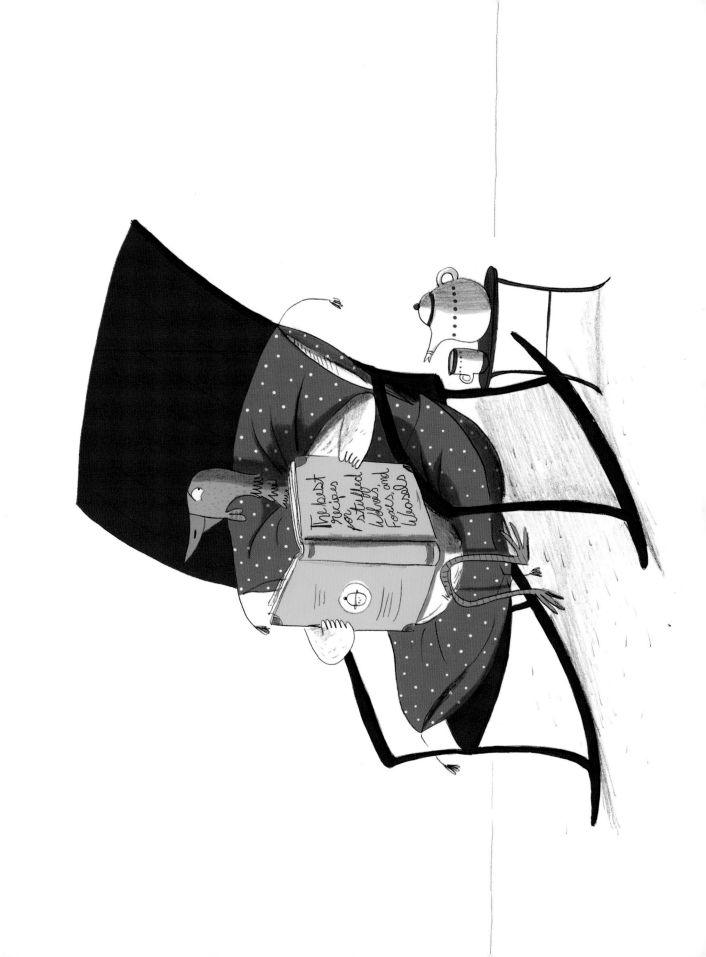